MESILLA

by

ROBERT JAMES RUSSELL

DOCK STREET PRESS
SEATTLE

www.dockstreetpress.com

www.dockstreetpress.com

ISBN: 978-0-9910657-4-5

Printed in the U.S.A.

It is better to have less thunder in the mouth and more lightning in the hand.

—*Apache proverb*

MESILLA

NEW MEXICO TERRITORY, 1863

A DISCOVERY MADE

Deep in the coyote hole Everett Root stood alert with the dented Dance revolver in his blistered hand and breathed heavy as he studied the body hunched over at the end of the tunnel. He waited, candles nearly extinguished and casting long shadows on the rock, and sniffed: no sulfur hanging in the air. No shots fired recently.

Everett rolled the revolver around his index finger and holstered it as if he were some dashing and wily roughrider that had been wrangled into a Wild West Show. He coughed a bit then set his eyes on the heaped body again, scratching his chin. The ache in his leg gathered up again like a fist and he snorted out a dollop of snot from his nostrils. He walked toward the body slow, dragging his hurt leg along the twin timber planks that bridged across the mud and wet recessed puddles in the rock. He braced himself along the wall and with his good leg kicked the body over so it now lay flat, face looking up at the ceiling: eyes bugged out, tongue swollen and parting thin, blue-tinted lips. He lowered himself carefully to the floor of the mine with a deep grunt and quickly patted down the body, searching for wounds but finding none. Scorpion or rattler, he figured and leaned back against the wall, waiting to see if the creature would show itself. He held his breath for good measure then let it out with a long-gestated hiss.

Everett said, "Well, shit. Sorry for your luck. Anyways, if you don't mind, I'm going to hide out here for a bit."

He unwound a piece of stained red cloth from around the upper part of his left thigh and he dropped the saturated tourniquet into a soaked pile beside him. He took two fingers and tore open his trousers and beneath the breach lay a bullet wound that fizzled deep, the skin encircling the wound lipped out as if it had been disturbed by some plated tremor deep below. He thumbed at it curiously as if he had familiarities with human anatomy then recoiled from the shocks of pain that shot back. He coughed and cleared his throat and squinted his eyes at the hole, imagining he could see the top of the stunted round glistening, and he wished he had dug the thing out in San Agustin when he'd had the chance.

He then reached out to the miner's boots. He sized them up and, too small, felt his way along the corpse, grimacing with hurt. Everett took a smudged hand and turned the man's head from side to side, gripping it along the jaw with the charm of a grandfather admiring a boy.

"Sunnuvabitch!" He guffawed and looked around for encouragement as if he had hallucinated an audience that likewise enjoyed his clowning and then let the head flop back onto the rock. "From the right angle, you look like my brother Jesse!"

He coughed again and rummaged through

the large pockets of the man's overalls and pulled out a small pocketknife with a pewter handle that it folded back into. He unfurled the blade which was dinged around most of the edge but the tip still pricked hard into the whorl of his thumb so he collapsed the knife and slipped it into his shirt pocket. Digging further he pulled out first a piece of folded paper that had browned along the edges then a large waxed piece of parchment which he spread out over his lap. In the dim light he examined it and it appeared to be a map of the area with hashes penciled in and around the mountains he was currently in. He didn't know what the hashes represented but by his best guess they marked failed claims. There was a longer scratch that portended to what might be a homestead a few miles off. He traced his finger along a ridge of the Organ Mountains then down through the scrublands until he hit Mesilla and he tapped it twice as if to make sure it was no phantasm of his mind. The edges of the map flayed and he took his thumbnail and chipped off dry mud from the lower left corner which revealed the words *John-son's California, Territories of New Mexico and Utah by Johnson and Browning 1860*. He stroked his hand over the dulled reds and yellows and greens that covered it and imagined they had been brighter once. Wondered how long it had been.

He set the map aside when he noticed the claw hammer slung along a leather belt askew at the miner's hips and he fingered the splintered handle and the iron cheek felt cool against his skin. He then set about unfolding the note and turned it in his hands, fascinated by the theatrics of it, and he held the paper close and squinted at the longhand words. He spotted a thick candle jammed onto an iron rod that had been wedged into the working face near the body, the flame nearly wicked away. Then he angled the paper in such a way that the remaining flicker of yellow light illuminated the page. He licked his lips and ran a hand through his greasy hair and glanced to the entrance of the shaft a ways to his right, waiting again for proof of his solitude. He focused on the extravagant loops staring back at him and enunciated with all the precision he could afford.

My dearest Bob,

I know you ain't seen me for a while now but I just wanted you to know I'm doing alright. And I'm really proud of how good things are going for you now that you working the land for the colors.

I don't know if you forgot or not, but my birthday was last week. And now that I'm fifteen years Ma's making me work down at William's store when I can. I'm meant to earn some extra money on account of Pa's arm being shot off by Mexers. I hope your still planning on saving up to come marry me and build me that house you told me of. And I never did tell anyone what happened between us and I never would. Anyways, I wouldn't risk getting you in trouble on account of me.

I hope this letter finds you well and I hope you can take me far from here soon and we can live forever together somewhere nice.

With great love,

Charlotte

Everett smiled and carefully folded the note back up and set it aside and exhaled loudly. "You scoundrel, Bob."

He looked up to the jagged ceiling dug out by erosion and the skilled hands of men and then counted the lateral wooden girts that had been placed at intervals of the shaft that braced the walls. Everett then tried to calculate how long Bob had been working the coyote hole and his leg resounded with another flirt of sharp hurt and he took the knife out and opened the blade. He looked back to the candle and thought maybe he would try to dig the bullet out now and saw how infection had spread up his thigh and neared his groin, the skin tender and tinged red.

Everett grunted and rested a hand on the rock

behind him and rose carefully. He panted for a moment with the knife still poised and he turned toward the body then heard a thunderous recoil echo back from somewhere outside, bouncing off the walls of the mine. He stopped and arched his back and the hair on his neck stood and he pursed his mouth so as not to produce any sound. The reverberation had deteriorated and he couldn't quite decide if it was thunder or a rifle shot. He thought he had lost him days ago.

He felt his nerves give and his heart raced erratically and he hobbled to the body, ignoring any better judgment to rest. He bent down and took the man's sweat-stained shirt and ripped a thick strip off, cutting the end free with the pocket-knife, and he tied it tight around his thigh. He winced as he double-knotted the bandage and then he noticed a tin ore bucket resting beneath the candle soaked in shadows.

A bit of rock collapsed near the entrance and he anxiously looked down the angled shaft where it glowed from the midday sunlight and then back to the body. His throat was dry and the new bandage provided a bit of release from the pain as he lurched forward. Then he reached into the dark tin bucket and pulled out a large and blocky hunk of silver ore that glimmered in parts from the candleglow.

Everett took his thumb and scraped dust off the surface and deliberated on the worth of the ore, then reached back into the bucket and pulled out a Colt 1851 Navy. The grip had been worn away and the steel of the frame and barrel were dull and tarnished. He broke open the cylinder and counted two rounds and then jammed the gun into his belt. He detailed the scene as he lingered and noticed an iron chisel peeking out of a fissured line of rock and an old shovel lying near. Satisfied he had scavenged anything of value from the place, he hopped on his good leg along the planked runners. They creaked and swayed in addled piles of mud as he moved awkwardly and he emerged along the entrance of the cave and pulled his Dance out.

The flat and polished-silver frame sat in contention to the pieced walnut grips and the brass trigger guard glistened in the afternoon sun as he knelt and rested it along the ground next to him in preparation for some ambush he figured was imminent.

He squinted his eyes as they adjusted to the flood of light and surveyed the scrubland: beige and brown hills dotted with olive green coursegrass and juniper and bands of creosote and beargrass that flattened out and continued on until devoured eventually by the horizon. The sky had lit up a brilliant blue as if to mock his predicament.

Everett stood back on his good leg and thumbed the hammer and called out, "George, that you out here? Can't we stop this, then?" He waited and listened to the wind as it ravaged the mountain slopes and the insect hymns that carried on for miles. "Or am I just talking to my damn lonesome?"

He visored a hand to his brow and searched the shadows of nearby privet yet to bear fruit, then slowly stepped onto the graveled slope that ran down to his horse that stood posted where he had left it. He stood tense until he was sure nothing had stirred in the distance, musing that maybe he had been on the run for too long, and he distracted himself from the specters he created by looking at the ore heavy in his hand. He rubbed his forearm against his cheek where sweat beaded and there was dried blood, thick like jam, along his brow. He smiled at the ore and rubbed the surface clean and he began shoveling his way down the steep slope past a bouquet of mesquite.

He reached his Morgan horse and placed the silver ore in a leather haversack that slapped against the animal's loins and he gripped the horn and pulled himself up with a considerable amount of pain. He took his old frock coat lying flat along the rear housing and placed it over his shoulders and it hung long and tattered at the cuffs. He then reached forward to a black fur-felt Kossuth whose hat-cord was tied to the front rigging ring and he placed it on his head. He scratched his chin and hocked up a wad of phlegm he intended to spit and then a rifle-shot rang past him and struck the gravel slope to his left, casting pieces of stone and dirt to dance like fire embers.

Everett heeyawed and clicked and dug his heels deep, slinking low in the saddle as he fled. He rose up a winding path back into the mountains and looked back only once to see where he was but the glare of the fading sun was strong in his eyes and he couldn't see his attacker as he raced further into the hills.

A SURVEY OF STOLEN GOODS

The next morning Everett walked down a hillside from the mountains leading his horse by the
reins. He had run a zigzag path the night before
until he exhausted the Morgan and then took a
position against a sheared cliff face that looked
out into a small valley surrounded by a grove of
thickly tangled cane cholla and blanketed with
needle-and-thread grass. The valley had only one
entrance that he had guarded like some stern des-
pot. Not wanting to light a fire and announce his
station, he had only slept for thirty minutes the
night before, shivering under his thinned coat and
dreaming of all the ways the silver could reignite
his life, could give him another chance.

He pressed on further from the hillside, stopping at a small creek that snaked down through the parched ground that was more mud than water and he let his horse drink while he inspected the map again. His detour had ousted him too far north and east of the Organs and now he'd have to cut back through. Everett clicked his teeth for amusement as he computed his new trajectory west and south and he looked for any mention of a trail or road through the mountains. He found none but felt optimistic that he was about a day's ride from Mesilla and he folded the map again along the worn creases and placed it back in his shirt pocket. He took out the miner's stolen pistol and broke open the cylinder again and double-checked the two rounds and tucked it back into his belt. He ran his fingers over his own large holster and stalled on the basket-weave pattern and then on the walnut stock of the gun as if he was anticipating a duel.

He yawned wildly and scratched the back of his head where it met the neck and bent down to the stream. He lifted a handful of the gray water to his head and spooned it over and slicked back his hair. Then he took another cupping of water and slurped it greedily and then sat along the bank and watched his horse which had taken to grazing on a sweep of hoary feather grass. He unwound the bandage from his leg and dipped it in the creek and wrung it out. Red water sifted from the dressing and he wiped it along his forehead which revealed a deep gash that had begun to scab over. He reapplied the covering to his leg and it was cold against his torn skin and he sucked in air through his teeth as if it deterred the stinging.

Through the late morning heat Everett's mind wandered and he thought of Leta wrapping her thin yet hardy arms around him but soon the memory shifted and distorted until it was George Lynn Hany staring back, guns drawn and fire screaming from his mouth, and the resulting quarrel that took place in his head was too much for that hour of the day so he focused instead on the distance, the shapes of nature, a trick he had been taught by his mother in his youth. Beneath the brilliant blue sky the peaks of the range rose around him as if escaping their earthly prisons and they were sidled by small trees and shrubs he didn't know the name of that stopped at a certain altitude until only bare rock jutted forth in long crooked pikes.

A breeze danced above him and for a moment, with his eyes now closed, he felt calmer, more relaxed, yet deep in his mind Frisco came bounding out and he imagined being in that house again, hatching plans with George to take the gold and what they planned on doing with it and how many men were stationed and the feel of the rocks in the street leading to it under his boots. Everett could feel the heat again on him and he was grinding his teeth now thinking of how it all ended and he pulled out the pocket-knife and extended the blade and splashed water on it before thumbing it clean. He admired his reflection in it then saw the scraggly beard that had supplanted his jaw. He wet his face again thoroughly and took to peeling off layers of the hair with the knife one stroke at a time. He cut himself repeatedly and left a twizzled mustache and when he was done he splashed water on his face again and it burned like fire, his neck dotted with blood.

He stood and looked out into the distance and he limped to his horse and caressed the haversack that held the silver. He pocketed the knife and looked out onto the landscape as he swallowed down a great wave of pain. The vista would be even prettier had he been there under better terms. He took off his coat and held it up and traced the mementos of battle, fingering where grapeshot had ripped through the cape and noting the splatters of blood that formed garish patterns where an elaborate sleeve-braid used to reside on the left cuff. He laid it over the horse's shoulders and oriented himself in his intended direction and he looked out on the brown rangeland and felt very tired.

A RESPITE

Everett had been riding for hours when sleep began to take him over in the saddle and he slapped his face to stay awake and calculated by the sun that it was deep into midday. He patted the Morgan's thick neck, coating his hands in the lather that had built up. "Alright," he said. He turned and looked back out at the expanse they had traveled, at the dust they had kicked up and the endless scrub they had left behind and yet still continued on before them and he smiled. "I think we're alright now."

He approached a young Emory oak whose branches cascaded out like a hundred tentacled arms and he tied the horse off and propped himself up against the knotted bark. He unholstered his heavy revolver and laid it on his belly and he fell asleep under the shade of the bell-shaped tree.

He awoke two hours later when his horse began to bray wildly and stomp the ground as if it were dancing to an unheard melody. Its eyes were whaled back so the whites shown and its mane stood up on its own. His senses still percolating, Everett wiped his eyes clean and felt a great pressure behind his nose. The ache had been gathering for days and for a moment he felt his face and thought he was conscious of someone else's body, remembering after a minute further that he had previously shaved. It was then that he grew alert to his horse's alarm and he heard the crackle of a rattler's tail and he spun and saw the snake coiled at the side of the tree, the diamond-shaped blotches running the length of its spine mesmerizing.

Everett jumped back as the snake lunged and its fangs nicked the heels of his boots as he landed. The snake reloaded for another attack and Everett stomped down hard on its head, repeating this action until it thrashed in place and was no more. He slumped back against the tree in the windless heat and breathed as though the air couldn't come fast enough. He was sweating profusely and wiped his brow clean with his shirtsleeve then bent down and sawed the snake's head off with the pocketknife and then unfurled it lengthwise and marveled at its span and girth.

He waited until dusk and he scouted the area on foot until he could no longer take the pulsing of his hurt leg, and he returned to the oak and felt comfortable that he hadn't been followed. He set to making a fire and skinning the snake, slicing the meat into finger-length strips, and then cooked the flesh in a small and near-smokeless blaze. He ate until he felt fat and bloated from the meat and gathered a handful of acorns still clinging to the tree and cupped them between a pair of grey rocks that ringed the fire until the outsides of the nuts had seared. The roasted perfume reminded him of his youth and he peeled the largest of the acorns and bit into it, finding it sour and tough.

He finished it for the nourishment and pocketed the rest.

He limped around the camp to keep the blood flowing regular and he found a snapped bough nearby that split at the ends. He inserted the sheath of the knife into the split and held the blade out into the fire until it glowed white-yellow around the edges. He hopped back to the saddle and took out a small tin flask and sloshed it around. It was nearly empty but he took it back to the fire and opened the tear in his trousers wider with his hands, pouring the liquid over the wound and he growled at the twinge. The knife had cooled some and clenching his teeth he began digging into the flesh of his thigh until he had carved his way around the expanse of the lodged cartridge and he began prying the thing up until it popped out like a cherry pit.

Night had settled fast on the rangeland and its dark shroud approached like a train. He picked up the crinkled acorn shell and examined it and chucked it out into the brush. He then rewrapped his leg and piled a mound of sand on the fire to squash it out and he dropped into a deep and tormented sleep.

A CHANCE ENCOUNTER

At sunrise Everett awoke and he drank cold tea
made from the leathery green oak leaves. Pink
light covered the scrubland in great spears that
had yet to reach his position which was still
soaked in the dampening night. The Morgan was
already set to grazing and he wandered to it and
brushed its side in long strokes as it flicked its tail.
He avoided gazing at his leg and bit his jaw together hard as if to sate the gods of pain, as if to
give them something to let him make it just a bit
longer. Between sips of the cold tea he studied the
coming light and the hills out near the horizon
began to take form: his mother lying in the bed
dying of consumption, spittles of blood curtained

along the contours of her sunken face and chest. Reverend Hasbrouk took him by the shoulders after and told him he was on his own now and he had no business being here and gave him twenty dollars and directions to a farm that'd hire him for labor. Years later he found the Reverend taking residence in his mother's house and utilizing her own things as his own and the two tussled in the street over how Everett was booted out. He ripped the Reverend's collar off and saw that he was just a man whimpering in the mud and dirt, begging to be spared. Everett beat him not only for that but for everything and left never to come back, never thought about it again until this moment, the pink bands of light spreading out before him holding him accountable to memories he'd tried to suppress and drink away years previous.

He finished the tea and packed his things and rode through the morning, attentive to any sudden changes in the landscape where a man might be able to hide, and he felt ready if the course of action presented itself. The left side of his abdomen had become sore and he felt a tightness when he inhaled, another complication from his previous conflict, and he held no doubts that at least one of his ribs had been broken.

Further north he pressed on over the buttressed base of the Organs and through infestations of sagebrush, slow as not to twist the Morgan's pasterns on loose rocks or exposed stems and roots. Behind him heatwaves rose from the ground producing confusion, apparitions he was careful not to give in to. At all times his hand was on the Dance. Fingers alternating against walnut and steel.

About midday he discovered a wagontrack worn down to soft earth the color of biscuits that snaked back west up and through the inclines of the mountains which he calculated would eventually spit him out onto the great flood plains northeast of Mesilla. He smiled and stroked the Morgan's great brown mane and they began the trek, eventually coming across two sets of naked footprints in the dirt and mud, but he didn't stop.

He made himself aware of his surroundings as he rode, practicing his draw and repeatedly turning to speculate on where they'd been. He passed by tracks of wolves and then came across a thick strand of perfumed creosote bush set between a narrow pass of land embanked on both sides by inclines. As his horse pressed on he squinted and saw black smoke willow up beyond the last of the soldiered shrubs. Everett ran his hand across the knurl of his gun and he stalled near a thicker expanse that shaded him from view.

He waited and listened and heard a scream belt up and then a carnivorous and mocking baritone laughter follow quickly behind. He moved his horse forward behind the next column of creosote and from his new vantage he saw a small cabin aflame. Out from the rear circled a thin girl in an oversized coat being chased by two Apaches dressed like Texans, their faces painted with dark soot and the braids of their hair winding down along their shoulders and bouncing as they moved. They danced and chased her and let her believe for a moment she could escape and then the closest of the pair tackled the girl to the ground. The second danced around like a drunk as the first mounted atop her and hit her hard in the jaw. She screamed and kicked and he held her hands down. Everett watched the scene dramatize before him, his eyes like dark stones set deep within the earth.

After a moment he clicked at his horse and double-backed through the grove and when he emerged he was at the rear of the cabin and clear of it all. The smoke was thick and smelled like a smithy and it stung as he sucked in air and swallowed down a succession of coughs that tried to rise up. He steered his horse around the side of the cabin and looped around back and when he came upon the Apaches his horse snorted loudly and alerted them to where he was.

The Apache that had been dancing was the first to react. He reached to his belt and attempted to pluck a revolver from it but Everett pulled out the miner's Navy and let out a shot that rippled into the Apache's head, striking him through the cheek. He fell to the ground dead and amid screams from the girl the second Apache rose up and howled and Everett fired the last shot of the miner's pistol and struck the Indian in the throat. He collapsed to his knees and hugged at the wound with his hands as if he was praying and the blood came like water from a spigot. Everett threw the gun down and clicked after his horse and circled the fallen man. Then he slowly took the long and heavy Dance from its holster, taunting the dying Apache, and fired another shot that struck him in the head.

The girl stood and her eyes were sunken and bagged with dark rings and she whimpered in disbelief. She looked up to Everett and dusted herself and her coat that looked as if it had once belonged to a barrel-chested man and she took one of the oversized sleeves and wiped the blood from her mouth. Everett was a handsome man in the most exotic and foreign of instances, with dark and brooding eyes deep set under thick brows and lips that bowed down then dipped up at the corners as if he was trying his hardest to charm nature in its entirety. He had a hand resting at his waist and thumbing the lip of his dark slacks, his other hand fidgeting in place as if it was hatching its own schemes. He was covered with a thick layer of riding dust, and underneath his ratty frock coat he wore a simple dark suit jacket and matching waistcoat, his gunbelt slung angled along his hips, the worn grip of his revolver poking out and waiting for his generous grope again.

"Thank you, mister. Thank you kindly. My name's Erin Sunderland."

Everett turned his head and spit a thick string of expectorate and eyed her warily, sweat forming at his palms and if his leg ached at that moment he chose not to show it on his face.

"You have no idea, mister! They was a'hollerin about and they was going to kill me. You really saved me, mister. What's your name?"

"Everett."

"Everett what?"

He turned in his saddle toward the creosote

then back to the cabin in flames and Erin again. "Everett Root. What was all this about?"

Erin wiped her face clean and her arms hung at her sides and she squinted her eyes to study the man who had saved her. "Thing is," she said, "can't really blame em."

"Why's that?"

"My pa was out hunting em, the Apache. Man came by some time back and said he'd pay fifty dollars a scalp."

"That so?"

"Anyways, Pa had no livelihood so went out and killed one."

"What's that got to do with this?"

"They were his brothers, they said. Came for vengeance."

"Well, where's your pa then?"

"Don't know. Said he was going to town but he's been gone a week. I suspect he's dead somewhere."

"And your ma?"

"I know she's dead. When I was a girl."

Everett sniffed and scratched his chin. "You're still a girl."

"I'm budding on womanhood," she said.

Everett smiled and pushed his hat down nearly to his eyes and re-holstered the Dance and thought about what would have happened with the girl if he hadn't intervened. He spit at the ground and adjusted his posture in the saddle. "Cabin's going up."

The two turned to watch the flames lick the walls and the lumber cry out as it cracked and peeled open. Erin said, "Well, shit." She watched him dismount.

Erin smiled and walked and stood next to Everett as he studied the cabin then removed his hat and wiped his brow clean. His black hair was pressed flat against his head and he emitted a musky aroma she wanted to suck in, his shoulders narrow but thick and his arms protracted and strong but lean as saplings. Everett removed his coat and jacket and rested them along the seat and tied the Morgan's reins to an old hitch.

"Help me," he said and tried to kneel by the first Indian's body but the pain from his bullet-wound had grown powerful again and instead he sat on the ground. He was a distance from the cabin and the smoke was thick and it fingered into the cloudless sky like a dark beacon. He swallowed and licked his lips and then studied the gray felted material that matted together to form the worn jacket. He touched it like a haberdasher might.

"With what?" Erin asked, arms at her side and peeling strands of hair from her sweated face.

Everett smiled and looked up into the morning sun and the warmth felt good on his face. "Seeing if they have anything of value."

"Looting, you mean," she said.

"Well, I don't believe either of these fellas plan on using whatever they have on em any longer. Anyways, I just saved your hide so how about you be a bit grateful for the life you still have."

"I'm grateful. Truly. Just never been so close to a roughrider before."

Everett laughed. "Just go check that one's

pockets and let me know what you find." He rested for a moment then began rifling through the coat, pulling out a few copperheads and a small jackrabbit totem roughly carved from piñon and a silver locket on a silver chain whose clasp had twisted and snapped. Inside there was a tiny daguerreotype of a plump infant cut and wedged into the oval-shaped cavity. He thumbed over the silver outside again, the relieved floral patterns pleasing, then held it suspended in front of his face like it had some spectacular authority over him. He analyzed it and then tucked it back into his palm and spit at it, rubbing it ferociously with two fingers until it gleamed and distorted his reflection like some mirrored caricature. He placed it in the breast pocket of his own coat.

He looked back at the girl now on her knees and carefully picking through the coat. "He won't bite ya," Everett said. "Promise."

She didn't look up but kept at it and pulled out from the pockets four rifle bullets all polished up as if just removed from a store-bought carton and a similar jackrabbit totem. She held them out to Everett so he could see and he shook his head no and she piled the items on the dead man's chest, careful not to let them roll off.

Everett stood and stretched and Erin did the same and said, "What now?"

"What now is I'm going to rest a while until I feel up to it then high-tail out of here and pretend none of this ever happened."

"Oh," she said. "What about me?"

"Don't rightly care," he said. "Maybe you can go searching for your pa."

Erin kicked the dirt at her feet and scratched the side of her head then her cheek. "There's a town back some miles the way you came called Blue Jay so I'll go there and tell em all what happened and see if I can track him down. He goes there to whore around. Friend of my ma has a place near there, always said she'd take me in if living with my pa got too irregular."

"Blue Jay?"

"Mining camp. Anyways, what else I got."

Everett thought about that and then realized she'd be headed back through the way he came and if by chance George happened upon her she might volunteer his position, might give away any advantage he currently had.

"Damn," Everett said and turned to her with his hand on the Dance. "Can't let you leave, turns out."

"What do you mean? Why?"

"Thing is, can't have you telling anyone about me. About where I'm headed."

Erin looked at his gun, eyes wide, and she clutched herself with the big draped arms of the jacket. "You going to kill me?"

"I'm no animal," he said and fetched some rope from the Morgan. "Suppose that means you'll come with me but I'm only headed to Mesilla and I'll deposit you there."

"Mesilla."

"As good as Blue Jay. Maybe better."

"And if I say no? If I refuse?"

"You seem a smart one. That right?"

"Yes."

"I think you'll oblige."

Erin kicked the dirt again and looked at the cabin then back to the grove of creosote then extended her arms. "Never liked it here much. Pa envisioned himself some great communicator with nature but we always had it tough."

"Consider this a fresh start then," Everett said. "You aren't a prisoner, you're just being liberated." He approached and roped her wrists together and knotted it in the middle and he wrapped the lead around his shoulder three times.

Everett carefully lowered himself back on the ground and winced. Erin said, "Whoever it is that's after you, they do that to you?"

"Do what?"

"I'm not stupid. I can see your leg's hurting."

"It's alright. On the mend."

"Alright," Erin said and lowered herself near him.

The cabin took to burning and the roof collapsed in on itself within half an hour and they watched in wonder as the Morgan paraded and rummaged through a stray clump of tussock. Everett dragged Erin with him as he scouted the area and followed a path that continued past the cabin through a narrow precipice that spilled out onto the flood plains. He leaned against a copper-colored hill of rock and vegetation at the trailhead and took the map out again, tracing his finger from where he presumed he was currently stationed. They would head south from the flood plains and then cross the Rio Grande at its most narrow and then he'd be in Mesilla.

Everett soaked in the panorama and pondered on how far he had come and how far he still had yet to go and hoped the girl Erin wouldn't slow him down too much. They were nestled between peaks of the Organs that rose like tortoise shells from the earth, humped in sloping arcs and generous inclines into rounded peaks, thick with sycamore and ash and cottonwood.

He folded the map along the edges and returned to the cabin leading Erin by the rope and drank water from a shallow well that tasted like iron. One of the Apaches had a rawhide canteen and he filled it up with water and replaced his pocketknife with a large Bowie variety that the other Indian had hidden in his boot while the girl looked on in marvel at his actions. Everett tucked the knife against the back of his belt and then checked both their guns. The sights were set crooked and worthless and he tossed them into the hillside where they landed with an echoed thwack. He saw an old Saratoga trunk that peeked out of the doorway of the cabin and with the girl's help they dragged it out before it could be ravaged by the flames, but he found nothing inside but old garments and the mildewed smell of age.

Everett coughed as he stood studying the trunk and the girl's outline through her coat, satisfied he had looted anything of value. She had remained quiet, perhaps understanding the severity of the scene now, following him like some lost dog doing what she was told. He tucked the map in a large pocket of his frock coat and took the silver ore out of the tied haversack and washed it with well water until it was lustrous and youthful in its appearance. He watched Erin eye the mineral and she couldn't help but speak again on the subject.

"Silver," she said. "That what they're after?"

"Who's they?"

"You said bad men are after you."

"I never said men, no."

"One man?"

"One man can be deadlier than many. You get too many together and everyone wants to have an opinion. One man answers to no one but himself and won't rest until he gets what he's owed."

"And he wants that silver?"

"Silver's not in contention," Everett said. "It was a lucky find. Going to cash it in when we get to Mesilla. You behave I may even give you a ration for your troubles." Erin smiled. "But first hand me that shirt I pulled from the trunk, will ya?"

Erin obliged and handed it over. "Was my pa's."

"Well, I'll be putting it to good use," he said.

He caressed the jarred surface of the ore with his rough hands and then with the Bowie knife sawed off the left sleeve of the shirt, tugging at the threaded remains until it ripped free at the seams. He then sliced the fabric down the center that opened the shirt to a large piece of fabric and then he cut the leather strap off the canteen. He then cut a small hole at each end of the sleeve, placing the ore at the center and wrapping it. Once it had been covered fully and wound tight he needled the leather strap through each of the small holes and knotted it at each end. He tested if it would hold by putting weight on it and it held up fine and looked like some sort of vulgar swaddling hanging at his side. He placed the strap around his neck then tucked it back into his shirt.

"You like to keep it close to your skin, don't you," Erin said.

"Ain't anything like miner's eyes or nothing," Everett said. "Just don't know what's waiting for us. And, see, I only had half a plan before I came upon the silver. This here's integral to my exodus and I can't fathom being parted from it."

He let the Morgan continue to graze and he hopped back with Erin in tow to the first row of creosote bush and lowered himself as he grimaced at the pain like a stage-actor might. He shifted in place until he had worn a comfortable seat in the scrub and they had the perfect view of the house turn to kindling. He unwound the bandage from his leg and it stuck to the wound, the fluids thick like honey.

A rock wren flapped noisily above and it called kereekereekeree at the fire that roared, seemingly dissatisfied with the intruders. Everett diverted interest from his hurt leg and squinted as the sun rayed down brightly and with one eye shut he followed the bird and its great-arced pattern until it disappeared beyond the ridges that humped up behind the cabin. He bit at his thumbnail until a chipped piece flicked off in his mouth and he spit it at his side.

Erin took to picking pieces of grass and tossing chipped red rock from the earth that landed with almost no noise in the distance. Everett mumbled to himself and looked back down to his leg and propped open the tear in his trousers. The skin around the wound had become darker and the sepsis trailed further up his thigh. He could barely touch the infected area without recoiling from considerable hurt and he held up his fingers and counted them down one by one until none remained, each a token of days past.

Everett's mind raced and he damned himself for being too cautious in Las Palomas. He regretted not facing George then over what he had done, being done with this all. But something in him told him to run, that the fury George had brought would never end and there was life yet to go on, so run he did.

"How bad?" Erin asked leaning over and looking at the wound in his leg.

"Told you," he said, "on the mend."

"I can help clean it," she said. "If you want. Helped my pa whenever he got scraped up so I know what I'm doing."

"Appreciate it, but I'm alright. Anyways, I'll get all fixed up in Mesilla."

"Mesilla."

"Yup."

Everett took an acorn from his pocket and bit into the flesh with his incisors and then began to peel the russet-colored skin away from the point of insertion. He chewed a sizable piece and it was bitter and he swallowed it largely whole. He looked back at Erin and saw her looking at the ground and then offered her one of her own which she took and pawed in her hands for a full minute before biting into. He took the rawhide canteen he had flung over his shoulders and drank to dilute the taste of the nut. The water gave off hints of whiskey that had been stored there previously and it burned slightly as it pitched down his throat. He slung the leather strap of the canteen around his neck and wiped his mouth clean with his shirtsleeve then dried his hands along the breast of his shirt.

The cabin timbers crackled and turned red in

the centers while the rest charcoaled and a pop-
ping sound rose up from the rubble. Everett grew
bored with the combustioned demonstration before him and took to scraping off the blood that
streaked in filamented designs along his shirt with
his shorn thumbnail and he felt a respite wash
over him.

And then in that moment of calm a boom-
ing shot whirred past the pair and hit the ground
to Everett's right, boring into the loose soil as he
backed up against the narrow trunk of the creosote bush with great alarm. Everett sucked in his
breath as his mind spun and only then looked over
at Erin who seemed struck by stagefright. Everett waved her over and she joined him hunkered
against the tree and Everett put excess pressure
on his leg as he shifted positions and it started to
bleed again.

Another shot rang out followed by another
and then the Morgan whinnied and another shot
struck the ground in nearly the same spot as the
first, sling-shotting debris up, and he panicked and

looked around for its origin. Then he stood with as much grace as he could afford and mouthed for Erin to do the same and they bolted toward the wreckage of the cabin while the Morgan continued to bray and run in circles at its hobble, disoriented from the sudden incursion of noise.

Everett's strides were narrow and as he stilted forward with Erin at his heels his face twisted in agony and then he felt a daggered stab hit him in the right shoulder followed by the explosion of the rifle-round exiting the gun seconds later. The pain was severe and it spread and he tripped over himself and shoveled hard to the ground pulling the girl with him. He spit out a hash of saliva and dirt, and with his thumb and forefinger, he pinched his eyes clean.

Lying on his belly between the trunk and the cabin, the smoke was thick and near to the ground and sheltered him for the moment from the assault. Erin was on her back holding back fear as best she could, but even still her whimpers escaped and he could hear his heart thump wildly. He tried to press himself up as his body wracked in a collective contraction of hurt, and he fell back.

"Just wait here a minute on the ground," Everett said quietly then a cough tried to come up as he breathed in the black smoke and he swallowed it down best he could, letting only a burp exit. They lay still and tried to take note of the approaching steps of their attacker then Everett reached his right hand down until he felt the stock of his gun. He gently tugged and it came loose from the holster with what seemed like a cacophony of noise. He checked his flanks and broke open the cylinder not comforted by the three rounds remaining.

He rearranged himself on his side and peeked beyond the trunk to the grove of creosote then another shot hit the thin wooden siding of the trunk and tunneled right through, only just missing his arched neck.

"Wait just a damn minute!" Everett let his words resonate from the sloping hillsides and he waited with the hammer of his gun cocked. "How about we have a chat about all this, George, alright?"

He rolled onto his back and the bullet in his shoulder felt awkward and buried and it pained him. He squirmed some more and the handle-head of the knife he had tucked away in his belt pressed into his back like the root of a tree.

"You got me between shit and sweat here. Payback, I suppose."

Everett again awaited a response but got none. Erin was still whimpering at his side and his mind began to hum and formulate how he could extricate them from this predicament. He thought of ducking into the grove and returning fire but didn't know where the shots were coming from. Besides, he reminded himself: George was a crack-shot with nothing more to lose. Then he counted how many steps it would be to the cabin's front door. Most of it had been eaten away by the fire, leaving a charred breach that looked like some devilish and crackling maw. He glanced quickly to the concaved roof and then to the two anterior window-frames that had collapsed fully from the weight of the headers and tie-beams. The cabin was all but cindered ruins now and yet it might hold the key to their flight.

"Fine, George. Just fine." He turned back to Erin and said quiet as he could, "When you see me get up, you follow. Do exactly what I do."

Everett's palm sweated along the grip of his gun and he counted to three. Then with a great burst of power and speed he rose and Erin, eyes wide and mouth open, stood along with him and they ran as best they could toward the cabin. A shot flew past him, connecting with a piece of the shingling, chipping off flakes of wood just above his shoulder. He vaulted himself through the charred doorway and over a small mass of dark timbers then fell awkwardly onto the floor and then Erin came tumbling after, landing on top of him and knocking away his breath. He had landed on the wrapped silver ore tucked in his shirt and it dug into his already sore ribs and he howled like a wolf as he rolled her off.

Another shot pierced overhead and he opened his eyes slowly, biting his lip. "You alright?" he asked. She nodded but did not speak. "Need you to answer. You hit?"

Erin checked herself and examined under the coat and let out a long sigh. "Not hit."

"Good." Everett stood slow into a hunch to stay low and Erin mimicked him. He was caked in dark soot. He wiped his eyes clean with his palms, revealing pale flesh that ringed his eyes. He coughed and pulled himself up and began stumbling forward in the smoky room toward the rear, waving his arms to prevent himself from breathing more of it in and to help him see.

Lying around them were the charred remnants of the girl's life. He spotted a pair of leather brogans collected and melting by an old cast-iron cook-stove and a partially finished ornamental rug aflame along the edges close to the bed which also lay dark and matted from the fire. His boots echoed on the floor and his eyes stung from the drape of thick black smoke.

He coughed again and thought he was moving in circles until his waving hands thudded against the far wall. He heard the recoil of the rifle, sounding closer, as he strafed his hands along the wall until he reached a window that had not yet buckled. He lifted his shirt up onto his nose like a bandit's mask and pointed for Erin to do the same and he thumped the butt of his heavy gun against the glass. It shattered with a loud crash. Smoke and spits of flame rocketed out the new exit and he jumped back to avoid being scorched. Then he shaved the remaining pieces of wedged glass from the frame with the barrel of his gun and heaped one leg out and over the sill. He ran his hand along his shirt and felt for the silver and then clasped the trim with his free hand and pulled himself free of the house, falling onto his hands and knees into the dirt.

He remained there in that position while he finished a sequence of wild and arresting coughs; his eyes clamped shut and his tongue wagged helplessly and felt as if it might rip off from the root. Erin climbed out of the window now and lying there he extended a hand. She reached down and helped him up best she could. Standing, he wiped a streak of the black soot from his mouth as he tilted his head up to fully catch his breath. The house nearly backed up to the steep rock cliffs as if the whole grove had been chiseled away by hand, just enough room to maneuver a horse back here. Near them was the trail that would spill out onto the flood plain, covered from view by the burning cabin. He hadn't heard another shot and figured George was either out of ammunition or biding his time to see what mistake his prey might make.

Everett wiped his gun free of soot and debris with his shirt. He took in large gulps of the clear air but his ribs heaved with hurt and he coughed with every lungful he took in. He saw the Morgan kicking wildly at its hobble to his right, dancing and trotting near the Apaches' bodies and he thought of running over and riding off but then figured the gunman might be expecting that. He stood on his leg and heard his hip pop and he limped forward, the soot blowing from his shirt as he moved.

"Goddamn," he said. "Looks like we're going on foot."

"We can't," Erin said. "It won't take long for him to catch up."

"I can't get to the horse," he said. "Either one of us takes a step out from this house and he shoots us dead. He's an ace with that rifle."

"Who is he?" Erin seemed desperate now, the fear rising in her. "Why does he want us dead?"

"He only wants me. You're just part of this now. I'm sorry about that."

Everett coaxed Erin on and they stirred into the narrow trail flanked by red-brown inclines on both sides of the path and he grabbed the rock faces for support. He clutched his gun firmly and heard the kereekereekeree of the rock wren again. He glanced up into the blue sky as he lurched ahead but couldn't locate the bird. Every step ached worse than he had ever felt and Erin trailed behind and he thought again of Leta and then the war and all that he had seen and that he promised he would never dwell on. Up ahead, he reminded himself, were the plains that stretched for infinity and the river that snaked through infinity that would deliver him to Mesilla, would take him away from George and his sins.

A SALVATION

Everett peeled a black-red paste from his lips as he sped through the trail. His groin excruciated in waves and he figured it to be lead poisoning. He pushed through the hurt and eventually slowed his pace, confident that George took to rummaging through his belongings back at the cabin. He ran a hand through his hair and coughed a bit and the path eventually opened up into the flood plain, dotted with lone cottonwoods and sweeps of brown desert grasses. He stood briefly to navigate and spied the gray line of the Rio Grande about a mile out and imagined he could hear it in the distance. Mesilla was still further south but he noticed a road on the far side of the river that would take him there.

Erin had calmed and they drank water greedily before hiking down the steep slope and across the range, passing monuments of salt cedar and sagebrush and croppings of bouldered sandstone.

Everett marched on, glancing back to the pass like clockwork. His vision began to blur and he mistook shadows of dashing clouds overhead as armies of villains bent on doing him harm. He crept on as his headache worsened and soon he forgot his sentried errand. He kept low to the ground and stopped himself twice from collapsing completely, bracing himself on Erin for a while until he became too much a burden and then he'd rest against large rocks.

His limp had worsened and he stumbled upon wreckage of some ruined wagonette and used a long timber from the wagon-bed as a crutch until it snapped in half after only a short while. The sun was hot and without his hat or coat he felt the full effects of it on the nape of his neck.

Erin squinted in the sun and watched Everett's face twist. "So, he's the one who done that to your leg?"

"One and the same," Everett said. "Ran into him in Las Palomas a few days back. Ambushed me there. Don't know how he managed to catch me, but there he was, waiting."

"Well, he's long gone." Erin looked back at the pass and slowed her walk to be at Everett's side. "It's just the two of us now."

"Don't bet on it," he said. "That George is damn wily. A real damn trickster."

They had been walking for three quarters of an hour in an unintentional crisscross route through the plains and had been stopping every few minutes to realign themselves amid Everett's worsening condition, stopping at a large and rounded granite stone at the bank of the river.

Everett gently lowered himself into the damp mud and his body throbbed all over, the bullet buried in his shoulder shouting in pain. The rock gave him significant cover and a cool draft washed

over him. He began another succession of coughing fits and spit up blood at the conclusion of each.
Erin stood over him and then removed her boots
and waded in the water and splashed cold water
on her hands and neck. Everett's hands were shaking from his wounds and the hunger that plagued
him and he took out the last acorns and chewed
them, skins and all, while Erin's back was turned.
They were rubbery and sour and he felt vomit
come up in his throat but he managed to keep it
all down. He untwisted the canteen from his torso
and drank the rest of the water. Some of it spilled
down his chin and felt cool against his skin.

"Well, we need to wade across," he said, "or
we're stuck here until my man stumbles upon us
in due time."

The river bubbled and called loudly and the
opposite bank seemed a long way off. Everett had
to squint to keep it in focus and mulled on his
original intent to head further south, of finding
a bridge or a shallow sandbank closer to Mesilla
that he could easily negotiate, but he knew he no

longer had the strength for this kind of investigation. He looked back to the steep slopes behind them that ran up to the Organs and then to the pass, dark with shadows.

Erin sat in the mud and slowly put on her boots. Her face was clean and shone white in the desert light. "Thing is," she said, "there's a camp north of here. Called American Flag. Ain't much of a thing, but Pa said they're trying to get incorporated and they're here for the colors."

Everett perked up. "How far?"

"Four, five miles, I think."

"You sure?"

"Pa took me there a few times to ration up. Really, ain't much of a place. Just getting settled by folks this past year."

"It'll do," Everett said and rose using the rock as support. Erin stood near him and removed her coat and placed it along Everett's shoulders. He nodded, said, "Give me your wrists." She complied and he loosened the rope and removed the lead from his shoulder and dropped it on the ground. "Suppose you're free to leave," he said, "but I meant what I said about George. You're part of this now and you're better off with me."

"You're a wreck," she said, laughing and rubbing her wrists free of ache. "But it'll do."

"You get me to Mesilla and I promise you a cut of the silver."

"Your promises any good?"

Everett smiled and crutched along the riverbank until he found a downed cottonwood limb bleached white from the sun. It was dry in parts and he broke off the rotted end and tested its strength then hiked it up slowly under his arms, cradling it tight.

"Lead the way, darlin," he said. "Be my salvation."

A CAMP CALLED

AMERICAN FLAG

By midday the camp called American Flag rose up in the distance, plotted against the banks of the Rio Grande. A road had formed in the dust, worn by wagons and schooners, and Everett counted tents as they grew nearer, a few dozen canvas or rawhide shelters that reminded him of bivouacked soldiers waiting for orders. His strength had come back some with the heightened morale of seeing the camp but his shoulder still screamed with hurt and he knew he'd have to see the Doc here before they pressed on or there'd be no chance.

He cradled a hand over the ore which lay bunched along his side and every so often he'd lose his balance but Erin would catch him and right him for some steps until he could continue on his own. Just outside the encampment they approached a ramshackle barn that had been constructed in haste, little more than a converted storehouse on the outskirts of American Flag. Everett stumbled up to it and took the cuff of his shirt and wiped a circle clean in the thick dust that gathered along a sectioned window. Inside were heaps of old crates and pallets of grain sacks stacked tall as a man. His coughing had worsened during his walk and it felt more cavernous now, as if his body was trying to eject something deep from within.

"What is it?"

"Stores," he said. "As you said, expansion is coming."

Everett stood back from the structure and Erin along with him and they looked at the camp again: men tended to horses and he could see the biggest tents in the center which would surely house the gambling and the whores. He hoped too for a livery if they were lucky. Women and children played and chored in the rows and then he saw a corral of horses nickering to one another and eating the tussock that grew here in great bunches and wagons in the distance still covered in dust.

"Keep this coat tight on me," he said. "Keep some mystery about us."

Erin fixed the jacket along his shoulders and they continued on to the camp. Everett's boots had dried some but his feet were damp and waterlogged from cooling in the river at intervals and he could feel the skin on his toes begin to peel away from the saturation. His limp was extreme now and drank the vigor from his being and as he hobbled into American Flag they came upon two middle-aged men conversing. The first man was fat, his charcoal waistcoat seemed ready to burst. He wore a .36 caliber Pocket Navy revolver slung in a small holster at his left side. The second man was tall and thin and wore a dark Prince Albert double-breasted frock coat with abbreviated lapels and carried no gun. The tall man blushed and stopped mid–speech at the sight of the approaching pair and an awkwardness settled between them. Everett eyed them back and waved with one hand while pinning the coat closed with the other.

"Afternoon, gentlemen," Everett said.

"Howdy," the skinny man said.

"Can we help yuh with something, friend?" The fat man snorted and studied Everett and then Erin and he tipped his hat and the skinny man did the same. "Where you two coming from?"

"Me and my sister here run into some road agents a ways back."

"That so?"

"Mhm."

Erin wrapped her arm around Everett's and lifted her head up, said, "Two of em. Gave us quite a scare."

"Where'd this happen then?"

"Back in the Organs. A pass in the rocks. We was cutting through," Erin said.

The fat man pointed to Everett's leg, to his

noticeable ailments, highlighting the wounds he was already conscious of. "Land sakes, son. Are yuh alright?"

"That was my next question, if you all had a doc in the camp."

The skinny man played with his chin, said, "Sure do."

Erin cleared her throat. "Which way is the doc?"

"Center of camp. Big tent smells of piss and medicine."

"And yuh should know he don't do charity," the fat man said, studying the pair again.

"We can pay," Erin said and puffed her chest out. "We got the money."

Everett looked out past the men at the camp again, could hear a woman singing in the distance and let the sweet words coat his ears then remembered his place and looked behind him at the expanse of scrub sloped from the river up to the Organs in the distance painted in orange by the fading sun. The thought of George still out there waiting gave him a chill. "You got a color mill here?" he said.

"Color mill?"

"Yessir."

The skinny man thought hard and licked his lips. "What yuh mean is an assay office, right?"

"Yes, that."

"If you'll allow me, maybe yuh should go see the doc, get yerself all fixed up."

"I appreciate the sentiment, but I'd just like to know if you got an assay office is all."

"Son, there ain't no point cashing in if yuh ain't gunna be healthy to spend it."

"Yes, what's the hurry, friend?"

"Just the assay office."

The fat man exchanged a wayward look with the tall man and then motioned behind to a row of tents closer to the river. "Charlie Lamb's set up back thatta way. But he's only a small operation. We all are."

"Thing is, most of us just been out there a short while."

"Charlie's got a shipment of goods and things en route. Only processing small bits for now. But he'll take care of yuh, give yuh a fair price."

"That's right."

The fat man tugged at his ear and tried his best to attempt any form of civility and then coughed into his fist. "You been mining?"

"Yessir."

"Near here?"

"In the Organs, day's ride or so."

"And your sister, she mining with you?"

"She came out some days ago to visit when we got bushwacked."

"Oh."

"Where yuh from?"

"Carolina, originally."

"North or south?"

"South."

"Yuh with Sibley?"

"Was."

"The rest of yuh left last year."

"I know."

"Well, just sayin' we ain't aiming for any trouble, things have settled here now. Yuh ain't trouble, are yuh, boy?"

"No, sir. Just needing to get fixed up is all."

"I thought y'all went east to San Antonio?"

Everett kicked the dirt a bit and bit his lip and folded his arms about his chest, his coat and legs thick with caked soot and mud.

"I parted ways after Glorietta."

The fat man placed a hand on his hip and cleared his throat. Everett saw hunger in the stranger's eyes which he greatly wished to distance himself from. The wound on his leg started to pound again and his shoulder began to wrack and spasm. He shifted his weight uncomfortably and then heard the trill and familiar kereekereekeree of the rock wren. Everett smiled and stared up to the sky and the afternoon sun was heavy and glaring in his eyes as he saw the small bird whoop and twirl. Everett hooted in place, genuinely amused by the happenstance.

"Well, I'll be, gentlemen. I believe that bird

there's been following us for miles. You fellas ever seen anything like that before, a bird taking to a man like a dog?"

The fat man squinted his eyes and followed the bird in the sky and the tall man did the same. Then he smiled a bit, said, "I saw a man, oh, some twenty odd years ago with a tamed magpie. Louder than hell, that thing was, but smart. Could even make it talk when he wanted."

"But this bird ain't tame, though. I've never seen a wild animal like that take to someone before, is what I'm saying. It's odd."

"Yes, it is odd."

The fat man clicked his teeth and Erin felt they had had enough of their company so she tugged on his arm. "Alright, then," she said. "Thanks to you both for the help."

"Good luck to yuh."

Everett nodded and Erin helped him along and he studied the tents as he passed. A woman dawdled out of one with her young son and then saw the rough and beaten man and scurried back inside.

The makeshift aisles between the tents were thick with mud and shit and at the center of it all a trough of fresh water and various supplies and barrels were stacked neat and all the tents spread out around them like the baroque petal pattern of a fancy flower. The biggest tent had a banner stretched over the entrance that read *Treasure Chest* and outside were women with bare legs showing, smoking cigarettes made from sweet black tobacco. Everett longed to smoke and he hoped he'd be well enough to stop in later and barter and that maybe they'd have Old Towse on hand which he'd grown quite fond of in his travels north. On the opposite side of the square he saw what he figured to be the doc's tent closed shut.

"There," Erin said having spied it herself.

"I want to check out Charlie Lamb's first," Everett said.

"You can barely walk."

"I just need to know," he said, "if I can cash in here."

"What about Mesilla?"

"We're still going to Mesilla but if we can cash in and stock up here we'll stand a much better chance, don't you think?"

Erin nodded.

"Then I'll get fixed up. Promise."

Laughter emerged from somewhere nearby and he heard the muted harmony of a piano being played from inside the Treasure Chest as it came alive. Everett led Erin past the saloon and they emerged at the furthest row of tents that overlooked the river. The sky that opened up in the distance was festooned with gray although they knew better than to expect rain of any true sort. Everett noticed too a small raw timber bridge north of American Flag just wide enough for horses where the river was narrow. He nudged Erin and without saying it aloud relief washed over them both like holy water.

The assay tent was made of spotted cowhide with a square base and was large enough to stand a few grown men inside. There was a significant lack of décor and it took the pair a moment for their eyes to soak in the darkness. In one corner was a small adobe furnace, corroded and dirty, next to a long table with a handful of small molds laid out.

At the rear end of the tent, seated at an ornate desk, an elderly man glanced up from his papers and wiped his hands clean on his soiled white apron strung about his waist. He peered through a pair of small round glasses at the unfortunate couple.

"What…uh, what can I do for you?" the man asked.

Everett reached in his shirt and took out the swathed silver ore and peeled the leather strap from around his neck before setting it on the desk. He carefully took the wrapping off and then took a lurching step back, presenting the rock like a proud parent might a child. Behind him Erin studied the room and its few offerings the way a pioneer might newly tread earth.

"That's a nice piece."

"Yessir. I heard you're just setting up, but was hoping you'd be able to process a piece this size."

The old man spit on his thumb and rubbed a section of the ore and studied it close with the round glasses placed high on his nose. "Thing is, I'm expecting a shipment of things tomorrow, day after. Could take to it with what I got, but it's just me and it might take a while to process it. You know, to tally it up."

"How long?"

"Day or two."

Everett stood erect and ran a hand through his dried hair. His shoulder ached furiously and his groin felt as if it had been set aflame but he stood proud with his chest held triumphantly. A quick draft raked in that felt cool on his neck yet he held his affixed gaze to the silver ore on the desk, smiling and placing a hand along it again, molesting the surface with great tenderness.

"I can wait until midday tomorrow," he said, "then I have to press on."

"Everett," Erin said but he held up his hand

and glanced back to the old man who looked over the piece again.

"Where to?" the old man said.

"Mesilla."

"Yup, they'll be able to process it alright. Just stop by in the morning, we'll see what we can do for you. Unless you'd care to leave it with me over night."

Everett packed up the ore and slung it over his shoulder and they left. Back at the square Erin pulled him aside before entering the doc's tent. "Maybe we should wait? Rest here a few days?"

Everett stared out beyond her, back to the land from which they came that now seemed twice formidable from the comforts of civilization. "Don't have that kind of time."

"Because of the man coming after you?" She wrapped her thin arms around herself. "Ain't you think we're safe yet?"

"Anyways," Everett said, "you want to stay, you're welcome to. But I'm out by midday, no later." He marched into the tent and Erin stood there a moment longer, thinking about the offer, deciding that perhaps Mesilla would be good for her as well, and followed him in.

A FEVER DREAM AND A FIRE

Inside the tent it was crammed with hanging dried herbs and various bottles of liniments and creams and crates that had yet to be unpacked and it did smell of piss as it was foretold.

The doc, named Wilcox, agreed to repair Everett for a small chunk of the silver he chipped off out back with the use of an aged mattock. He wore a white shirt and waistcoat dirtied by both soot and dried mud. He had a long black beard that twizzled at the end into gray and wore small round glasses that he folded into his waistcoat pocket when he was making a point.

After some discussion Wilcox removed the bullet in Everett's shoulder and tended his wounds with the help of his Mexican assistant Lucio who spoke no English.

"No te quedes ahí parado," Wilcox said to Lucio while he dug the bullet out. "Detén este plato."

Lucio grabbed the scuffed plate that sat atop a nearby crate without responding and held it out as Wilcox dropped the blood-red bullet onto it with a plunk.

Erin stood by amazed at how quickly the doc had moved and while he tucked Everett into a cot in the back, she said, "See a lot of wounds like this? You seem mighty capable."

"Sure," Wilcox said then turned to Lucio. "Hay mucha gente estúpida por aquí."

Lucio laughed, said, "Seguro que sí."

"What'd you say?" Erin asked and clutched the silver tight to her and thought for a moment of grabbing Everett's Dance still in the holster slung along the back of a chair aside the cot in offense of this man.

"I don't ask questions, girl," he said and

laughed. "I'd have no paying customers if I did."

"Qué dijo?" Lucio asked.

"Dice que si les hacemos muchas preguntas a los pacientes," Wilcox said. "Le dije que ya estuviéramos muertos."

"Muertos," Lucio said and smiled and rubbed his hands together in amusement. "Dead."

Everett said, "Anyways, she's staying here tonight with me."

Wilcox looked at Erin. "That's fine," he said. "I got a place the other side of camp but Lucio stays here. Suppose he can bunk out front tonight."

"Sure."

"Suppose the two of you will want food, huh?"

"Yes," Erin said.

"I'll get Lucio to cook you up some beans and tortillas. He does em both real good."

"Thanks."

"Yeah, alright."

Wilcox wiped his hands on his waistcoat and clicked his teeth as if puzzling something. "You wouldn't be interested in selling your plot, would you? Seems to be the real thing, don't it? Anyways, you laid up like this, just thought I'd inquire."

"You come out here to mine?" Erin asked.

"Like everyone else. All this land, it's ours, you know."

"How you figure?"

"All this is our calling," he said and wiped his hands on his shirt and played with his beard hair. "We took it from the Mexicans, took it from everyone. There ain't anything can stop us. Ocean to ocean, we are meant to be here."

"Oh."

"Goddamn truth," Wilcox said. "We harness the wilderness here, make a town out here in the middle of goddamn nowhere. Now we're thriving, mostly. More and more coming out here to work the rock, find their fortune. All this was God's plan for us."

"So we're chosen?"

"We were, girl," he said. "Ain't no other way about it."

Everett propped himself up, cleared his throat. "And you ain't serving?"

"The war? They don't need me. Can't hit shit with these tired old eyes."

"Reckon there's always use for a doc."

"Suppose I could ask you the same. All us out here, we're a bunch of refugees don't want any part of it. Just trying to start new." Wilcox stomped his feet on the packed dirt floor and clapped his hands. "Now how about that mine of yours?"

"Sure," Everett said. "Alright. We'll talk to-morrow afternoon."

"Shit, that's wonderful. How far from here?"

"Day's ride or so."

"Well, damn." Wilcox looked at Lucio and smiled, his teeth straight but yellowed. "Nos va a vender su mina de plata, amigo. Seremos ricos."

Lucio smiled, said quietly, "Ricos."

An hour later while Erin ate tortillas mopped in beans stewed with spices she'd never tasted Everett fought off a fever and fitted through sleep on the cot. He had the Dance now in his hands along his chest, ore at his side. Wilcox had given him swallows of rotgut to ease the pain and Everett let the booze immolate his brain, hazing his thoughts into all that he had tried his best to suppress.

There was a morning back in Frisco when it all came together. It was hot and the two of them were posted in a dark alley adjacent the livery. George rubbed his sleeve against his scalp to wipe away some sweat and he glanced up at the bank, squinting hard in the sun and fixing his sights on silhouettes that glowed black in the light.

Posted in garrisons above Grady's saloon and Miss Margaret Fenniman's Wonderland whorehouse were a handful of plucky and galvanic men who had been recently deputized and placed at their posts to protect a shipment of Union gold en route to Arizona. The stationed minutemen were sworn in as agents of the law in case anything got out of hand in the absence of the soldiers, and in front of their proud and wide-eyed sons and daughters they were taken into the fold of the law, given explicit instructions to keep an eye out for any who might intend to deter the renewed and discontented Union government. They were given their choice of a handful of broad-blasting irons, nicked and worn Winchesters and an assortment of breech-loading shotguns and galvanized sixshooters that were eagerly distributed and fondled with great encouragement.

"Those men," George told Everett, who stood slightly behind with his arms crossed. "I know those men and those men won't die for that gold."

"That means those men know you, too, huh?"

"We were looking for a new start," he said. "Might as well leave Frisco in a blaze of glory."

Everett laughed and touched George's shoulders. "So we go in blasting?"

"Wait til dawn."

"What about the Calvary?"

"They're off scalping savages," George said. "Clearing the roads. Won't be back for a day, probably two."

"Just the two of us?"

"Mhm," George said, looking back at the

stationed men and the buildings and then turning and placing a hand on Everett's shoulder and
looking him square in the eyes. "Ain't no one else
I trust in this world."

When Everett awoke Erin was standing over
him, shaking him to.

"What is it," Everett said, sitting up. He
touched his forehead and it was damp and warm.

"Someone's set fire to the camp."

"Fire?"

"Doc came by, said someone lit a tent on fire
and then another went up with it."

Everett cleared his throat and then realized
the words that had been spoken and flung his legs
over the cot and he stood. "Shit," he said. "Not an
accident? You sure?"

"Someone said they saw someone toss a lan-
tern at one of the tents."

"We have to go," Everett said and grabbed his
boots and pulled them on his sore and swollen
feet. Erin watched him as he dressed and counted
the scars on his chest and stomach as he put his

shirt on. Everett buckled the holster along his waist and rotated his shoulder as if testing it out.

"How is it?"

"Better," he said. "But we really gotta get."

"Why?"

"It's him."

"The phantom?"

"Yup."

Everett wrapped the haversack with the silver around his neck and Erin dressed in her coat again and they slipped out past Lucio who stood at the tent entrance entranced by the great pyres burning at the edges of the camp. The sun was quickly fading and the sky burned deep red and Everett led Erin back through the rows amid screams of women and children crying out in the dusklight for their homes that were no more.

At the north end of camp they came across a small pen containing a Pinto and Appaloosa ranging for grass and saddles had been laid over the pen fence nearby. Everett waited and saw no one and assumed all had gone to squash the blaze so he gave Erin the Dance and told her to keep an eye out for a black man with fire in his eyes and that if she should see him to pull the trigger until it had emptied.

Erin stood waiting and could hear her own heart up in her throat. Nearby Everett saddled the Appaloosa who obliged him and after he was harnessed he called out to Erin and they rode together in the saddle away from American Flag over the raw timber bridge across the gray Rio Grande toward the deepening red, their backs to the blackness that raced to consume them.

A STORY TOLD

At sundown they camped at the base of a mesa that rose from the earth like a fist looking out over the plains that glowed golden as the sun disappeared beyond the Organs. Everett built a small fire and they sat eating the meat of a sinewy hare that he had found in one of the saddlebags. They could see the river a couple hours' ride from their vantage and American Flag lay somewhere north but completely obscured now and for a moment Everett felt safe. He watched as Erin ate greedily, her face stained with the grease of the meat, making little noises every so often as if to placate him.

"Anyways," she said, sitting back against the rock and wiping her hands on her dress, "I can't quite figure it out."

Everett finished chewing then picked a piece of meat out of his teeth and licked it off his finger. He looked out over the plains and folded his hands along his lap, could feel the Dance resting on his crotch. The hurt in his leg was so bad now even just resting was a pain. "What can't you figure out?"

Erin sniffed, said, "You. This. You ain't fixing to have your way with me and you're claiming to give me a piece of the silver when we get to Mesilla, and after every step you take you're looking back over your shoulder after some phantom you claim is haunting you and you alone."

"You've been at my side. You've seen those shots ring out."

"And the fire may have been just a fire."

"Maybe."

"But you don't think so."

"I do not, no."

"Well, whoever it was ain't here no more, that much is obvious. Who the hell even knows where we are? I don't, you don't. Sure as hell your phantom don't." She paused and cracked her knuckles. "Yet…"

Everett sat up and spit at the ground and turned toward her. She seemed even younger in the oranges and reds of the dancing flames, just some girl with eyes too big and hair that twisted down past her shoulders, with her whole life yet to attain. "Yet what?"

"Dunno. You got this man chasing you all over this county, further maybe, who knows. What's the reason for that, to drive a man to that sort of desperation?"

"How old are you?"

"Why's that matter?"

"Curious is all. You seem wise."

"I'd be wiser if you put the gun away."

"Gun's not for you."

Erin laughed, extended her arms to the plains as if in some grand gesture. "We're alone. Seems pretty obvious to me, but you can't seem to accept it."

"I'll accept it when we're in Mesilla."

"Got something there to protect you from this phantom then?"

"Told you, going to get myself fixed up."

Everett thought about Frank and wondered how he'd be welcomed. He was grateful he had stumbled upon Bob and the silver in case any bad blood still existed between them, in case he'd need to pay for their history to be re-chronicled completely.

Erin yawned but fought it back and admired Everett's crooked nose and she wondered if he had a woman somewhere. She felt a warmth in her belly that she knew not to linger on. "Buy yourself some new life?" she asked.

"That's the general idea."

"And if this phantom's still out there, hiding behind a tree, waiting to pounce on us, how's all that going to stop him?"

Everett leaned back against the rock. He rooted around at the ground and found a chipped piece of stone and threw it out down at the slope until he heard it crack against the hard earth. He said, "How old you think these rocks are we're leaning against?"

"Old," she said.

Everett smiled. "Suppose so. And I'm sure they've seen their fill of us humans quarrelling, huh?"

"Reckon."

"Never really changes then, I imagine. Everything that goes on with us. We change, I guess. Don't live in the caves anymore. But everything else we do, fighting, the chasing, all the killing, it all stays the same."

"You sound like a drunk going on like that."

"Drunks are wise. Stupid, but wise."

"My pa wasn't wise."

Everett sucked in a deep breath and let it out slow and instantly felt the pain in his leg coursing up through his abdomen. He wondered if the doc in Mesilla would be able to do anything more for him by the time they had arrived.

"I knew a man once," Everett said. "A good

man, a friend. See, I was a deserter." He waited, looked at her. "Not necessarily a good man myself. Not a bad man neither, but not a good man. Not like him. Anyways, we became friends, and we made plans. Well, I made plans, convinced him to go along with it."

"What plans?"

"Not the murdering kind."

"You fixin on being an outlaw? Gonna hold up a bank?"

"Don't matter now. Anyways, we spent a lot of time together, me and George and George's wife Leta. She didn't know what we were up to and that's how it should've been, but they took me in when I had nowhere else to go, and I was forever grateful." Everett cleared his throat and chortled and ran a hand along the rock, felt how it had been worn down over time. "And then I fell in love with Leta and she fell in love with me and something happened. I don't regret that, not at all. I regret doing that to George, but we had…"

"Ain't that what all men say? Their love is the

only love?"

"Some do, but I mean it. It was something there I never felt before. I know she didn't either."

"And George found out and that's who's chasing us?"

Everett stretched his legs and massaged them gently. He took the same hand and wiped his forehead down his face to his chin and left it there, surveying the horizon, the shadows and black shapes fingered along the earth among the darkness. He imagined being at the river again, following it to Mesilla and the weight of the silver being lifted from him as he cashed in. "She died," he said. "She was killed."

Erin cleared her throat, picked a piece of meat from near the fire. "I'm sorry," she said.

They sat in silence, soothed by the sound of night creatures making haste, searching for food, the quick flutter of bats overhead. Then, in the distance, the howl of a lone wolf, deep and guttural as it ascended to the heavens, echoed around them. A moment later two more rang out, replying to the call.

Erin looked at Everett who had his arms folded up at his chest, head down as if studying them deeply. She said, "When I was young my pa would tell me stories from when he worked a cattle ranch up in the Wyoming Territory. Wolves were always a problem, would always find some way of snatching up a cow, a young one, anything they could get. He always said the cleverest fox still isn't as smart as the dumbest wolf."

Everett looked up. "That so?"

"Mhm. Anyways, they had a few cowboys up there that hunted wolves good, half-Indians I think. But the wolves figured out the traps, how to avoid em, so they had to start using wolfhounds. These great big mangy dogs as big as a pony. So when the wolves would act up and kill a cow they'd take the dogs on these long trips. They'd be gone for days, and sometimes my pa would go. And after days of searching and hunting when they found the wolves, the hounds would chase em down until they were exhausted, tire em out chasing across the grasses and hills and separating em from the pack, then the cowboys would ride up and finish em off. Sell the pelts to some folk for twenty-five dollars each."

"Lot of work for a little money."

"Yeah. Lotsa folks wanted at least fifty, Pa said, but they weren't having it. Anyways, he always said it was a shame."

"What was?"

"The wolves outsmarted the traps, the first ones, because they smelled the people on em. Knew something was up. But the wolfhounds… the wolves didn't know their smell, didn't know what to make of em so they let em close, too close, before realizing it was all a trick. Then it was too late. It just seems unfair, like there wasn't any point to it all. Give em a cow every so often, let it all take its course."

Everett snickered. "Well, you feed em then they want more. Won't stay away."

"Maybe." Erin rubbed her boots together and scratched her face. "But ain't it our fault for interfering with things? Changing the natural order and all that? Tricking them to slaughter just seems mean."

"Just let things be, huh?"

"Sure."

Everett thought about Leta and could still smell her in the air, the feel of her skin on his rough hands and the way her hair always smelled as if it had just been washed moments before. He remembered her eyes most of all, almost too large for her face and when they'd lie together touching and stroking one another he would peer into them and see the parts of himself he didn't care for disappear completely and it would soothe him to his core. Then the image of George flashed before him, teeth showing and the blood on the bed, so much of Leta's blood, and so he stood and braced himself on the rock to prevent toppling over from faint.

"I'm going to piss," Everett said and he set the gun on the rock between them.

"Ain't you afraid I'm going to take your pistol

and hold you up in the dark here?"

Everett nodded, said, "No, ma'am." And he waited but wasn't sure for what and saw Erin smile sweetly and try her best to brush the hair out of her face. He smiled too and surveyed the land again before meeting Erin's eyes and she watched him recede into the darkness, hobbling slowly over the graveled earth that met the large mesa sides until he was gone completely into the void.

Everett couldn't quiet his mind so he kept on in the dark longer than he meant and when he turned back the camp was a good twenty yards away. He clutched his leg above the wound and grimaced then watched as Erin stood and stoked the fire with little kicks, adding small pieces of timber to it. He could he hear it crackle and devour the kindling with great hunger and she seemed in another world to him then, cast weirdly by the firelight, when a shot rang out and struck Erin, sending her back and down. It took a moment for the sound of the shot to reach Everett and he seemed to be seeing her go down in his mind in some tormented repeat, and when the echo of the blast made it to his person he ducked against the wall, bathed in darkness still, waiting for echoes to be chased off completely out on the scrubland.

Everett's heart beat fast and wild yet he waited, listened. It was a rifleshot, he knew that, but wasn't sure from where, and then, as if by instinct, he felt the silver at his side, cradled in the swaddle he had made for it.

After the gun noise settled he stood slowly then heard the faint sound of Erin's cries for help, low and deep as if it were not possible to raise her voice further. She was calling out to him, calling his name, each time striking him like a knife to the core of his already fractured body and he thought of going to her and helping her up and making off together, covered by night, but instead he felt the silver along his body and swallowed hard and thought of Leta's face and her voice so that he could no longer hear Erin's weeping and he slowly sidetracked down the mesa slope and mounted the Appaloosa and headed south and east toward the river until the camp was completely obstructed and with it all the promises he and the girl had shared.

A PAYMENT MADE

By late morning Everett woke atop the Appaloosa which had taken to a slow trot without his inter-ference. His face was chapped and reddened by the early sun and his shoulder was stiff and it had become pandemonium in his head hearing Erin's voice call out to him.

He took the patterned blanket strapped in be-hind the saddle skirt and wrapped it around his shoulders and up over his head. Before him the scrubland flattened out and in the distance great toothy grey peaks loomed overhead as if attempt-ing to pierce the cornflower blue sky. Beneath the range he could see the faint glimmer of Mesilla sheltered in the stony shadows. He perked up and tried to smile.

The Appaloosa began to fidget near midday. Everett was meticulous in checking his flank for his pursuer and, confident he was alone he led the horse back toward the river whose banks were green and thick with rabbitbrush and sagebrush, bluestem, willow and boxelder that cast long shadows over the gray water.

He let the horse graze as he lumbered carefully to the water and he drank until his belly ached. He lay back along the slope in the shadows of one of the hanging boxedlers and he let the green surround him, and for a moment all else seemed to fade. He tested the mobility in his shoulder and touched his leg around his wound which seemed to be taking to the liniments given to him by Wilcox. He wished he had the Dance and he fingered the empty holster at his waist, but he could see the white-capped mountains against the horizon, half a day's ride, the civilization twinkling below as if it were calling out to him and he smiled. He thought of Frank and then of all the ways in which he would disappear after getting fixed up. He pulled the swaddling from around his side up onto his chest and he peeled it open and studied the silver again. He spit on his thumb and rubbed it clean and still he marveled at its glow.

His stomach pained him with hunger and he chewed on a long strand of grass and sat up on the bank and searched in the shallows for small fish he might be able to pull up with little difficulty and then the Appaloosa brayed wildly and then calmed and nickered the way they do when comforted.

"Rabbit." Everett slunk against the bank of the river and flattened himself best he could and knew instantly the voice that had haunted his recesses. "I know you're down there so no use trying to pretend otherwise."

Everett sucked in his breath and waited.

George Lynn Hany stood up the bank with his polished Sharps rifle slung along his shoulder and with his other hand stroked the Appaloosa's neck and shoulders. Behind him his own palomino stood bridled and grazing. A significant ring of dry dark blood stained the right shoulder of George's shirt and he wiped his hands clean on his worn galluses then smiled. He pulled the stunted brim of his derby down along his eyes and cleared his throat. He could see the river from his vantage but not Everett or his exact whereabouts.

"You been leading me on quite a chase, Rabbit," George said.

"Don't you come down here," Everett said. "I'll blast you full of holes."

George laughed, said, "I know you don't have your piece, Rabbit. Found it with the girl. Shame about her."

"You shot her."

"I pulled the trigger but her downfall is on you. Everything you touch flares up, don't it, Everett?"

"You should just let me pass. Ain't you seen enough bloodshed?"

"I'm only after you, Rabbit. Then this hunger will be sated."

"Goddamn, George. I can't tell you anymore how sorry I am."

"You killed Leta."

"I was with her but you shot her. Just like Erin and all the others along the way."

"She was my wife, Rabbit. You gotta answer for that."

Everett looked out at the cloudy water flowing south then back to the mountains in the distance and he listened to the riversong. "I mourn her too."

"But you have no right to, do you? Anyways, it don't matter. Got my Sharps and you know I'm a crack shot. I say this is where it ends so take stock of where you're at, Rabbit. This here's your grave."

Everett said, "There's a world out there where we're still friends. Where none of this badness happened and we're living in Mexico, the three of us."

"Maybe," George said, "but you can think of something better."

Everett tucked the silver back in his shirt and

breathed out three times then rose up and jumped into the water. He could feel his boots sink in to the mud of the riverbed and knock against stones half-buried.

George watched him and steadied the Sharps and fired and hit Everett in the shoulder. Everett tumbled into the water and the bottom slipped from him altogether. He paddled violently toward the other side until he hit a strong current that began to lead him south, sending him nearer the mountains and Mesilla, nearer Frank and his salvation, and he felt the silver at his side chafing his skin and he looked back at George whose face had no reaction, no great joy or sorrow. Nothing.

George nodded to Everett and Everett paddled wildly and George steadied another shot that hit Everett in the neck that pounced him forward and down into the water. Everett could feel his body give way underneath him and he struggled to stay at the surface but could no longer pull himself up. He took great gulping breaths that flooded his insides and he panicked and swallowed the gray water and coughed and could feel his breath being squeezed from him. Everett saw in the great cragged peaks that now seemed to buffer the horizon Leta's face looking back at him sternly as the light went out of his eyes.

THE END

ACKNOWLEDGMENTS

A portion of this story originally appeared in slightly different form in the literary journal *BULL*—a hearty thanks to Jared Yates Sexton and Christopher Wolford for their confidence in me and my writing, and for giving me a chance to share this with the world.

Thank you to Ashley Strosnider and Francisco Velasquez for helping me with my Spanish, making sure it was up to par.

I'm also eternally grateful to Dane Bahr and everyone at Dock Street for their endless enthusiasm and the countless hours spent discussing Westerns and inspiration. Their wisdom and keen eyes helped make this what it is.

Thank you to my family and friends—I am so lucky to be surrounded by so many passionate people who see the world so differently, who support me and challenge me into working harder and being the best human I can be.

For all your unconditional love and support, thank you to my wife, Patty. She is a necessity for my sanity, she is my favorite critic, and her support means the world.

And thanks, too, to Elmore Leonard. I never met the man, but he is, unflinchingly, the reason I love Westerns. It's a shame that something so uniquely American has fallen out of fashion, and I'm honored to be adding my own story to the lexicon of Western tales.

R.J.R.